Tales from Netherwitton Wood

Written by
Matthew Davies

Illustrated by
Phil Woodsford

Just beyond the wheat field at High House Farm, near the village of Netherwitton, there is a small wood.

One morning as the sun comes up, there's a scratching and a rustling noise coming from a tree near the barn. From a hole in the tree out pops a nose, twitching and smelling the fresh morning air.

It's Ralph, the Red Squirrel and this tree is his home.

Ralph looks across the wheat field and sees something in the air. It looks small, but it's coming closer and flapping its wings. It swoops down and lands silently on a branch.

It's Ralph's friend and neighbour, Olivia the Owl, who lives in the next tree.

"Good morning, Olivia," says Ralph. "I wish I could fly like that."

"Why don't you try?" asks Olivia. "I'll show you. It's very easy, when you know how."

Olivia spreads her feathered wings, springs from the branch, and leaps into the air.

Gliding gracefully down she begins to turn and loops the loop before coming to rest back on her branch.

"You see?" she says. "Now you try."

Ralph feels nervous. He's never flown before. He spreads his arms as wide as he can and takes a deep breath. Plucking up all his courage he closes his eyes and jumps!

"Oh help!" cries Ralph as he suddenly realises that, while he is good at jumping and climbing, he isn't so good at flying.

"Don't panic!" calls Olivia, sensing the danger. She swoops down to catch Ralph on her back and fly him safely up over the tree tops back towards the branch.

"That was close," says Ralph. "Thank you. I think I'll stick to climbing, but wow! You can see for miles from up here. Hello Mr Blue Bird. Hello geese."

Just then there's a voice from inside Olivia's tree. "Bedtime Olivia. In you come." It's Olivia's mummy.

"See you later," Olivia says. "Have a nice day."

"Bye Olivia. Sleep well," says Ralph and then in a quiet voice, "It's a shame we couldn't fly together."

After a long day sleeping, the sun is beginning to go down behind the farm. Olivia hops out on her branch and sees Ralph scurrying up his tree.

"Good evening, Ralph," she says. "You really are good at climbing. I wish I could do that."

"Hello again Olivia," says Ralph. "Climbing isn't hard at all. You just hold on tight with your claws. It's just like walking, but you do it upwards, instead of along. Why don't you try it?" he suggests.

"OK," agrees Olivia. "I'll give it a go."

She holds on to the tree trunk and starts walking upwards with her feet, but her wings can't grip the bark and she falls.

"Ouch," she cries as she lands flat on her back. "I don't think I'm cut out for climbing," she says unhappily.

"Don't worry," Ralph tells her. "I'm sure there's something else we could do together instead."

"Yes," agrees Olivia. "We just need to think of something."

The sun is almost gone now and a voice comes from inside Ralph's tree. "Bedtime. Come and brush your teeth." It's Ralph's daddy.

"See you tomorrow," Ralph says.

"Goodnight Ralph," replies Olivia and she flies off into the evening thinking about how good a climber Ralph is.

It's the next morning and Ralph is up early. The friends still can't think of anything to do together.

"Let's go and visit my great uncle," suggests Olivia. "He's awfully wise and always has great suggestions."

The wise old owl lives in an oak tree, the biggest and oldest tree in the wood. Olivia and Ralph set off to find him and soon arrive at his home.

They tell him all about their problem. They tell him how Olivia can fly, but Ralph can't. They tell him how Ralph can climb, but Olivia can't. Then they ask him what they can do together.

The wise old owl thinks for a moment, then in a slow voice asks, "Why do you need to DO something together? Sometimes it's nice for friends to just BE together. Now, if you'll excuse me I must get back to my books."

The two friends head back across the forest to their trees, thinking about the great uncle's wise words.

Back on their branch, Ralph tells Olivia all about what he does during the day. Racing and climbing, burying acorns and forgetting where he's put them. Olivia laughs at his funny jokes.

Olivia tells Ralph all about her night time life. The adventures she has in the dark, flying high in the sky and swooping through the air. Ralph listens, amazed by her exciting stories. They talk and laugh until Olivia goes to bed.

And, as the sun sets, they do the same in the evening until Ralph's bedtime.

Printed in Great Britain
by Amazon